For Jake, who was there
in the mountains of Big Sur
for the very first step!
—A. B. M.

For Peter
—D. G.

SIMON & SCHUSTER BOOKS FOR YOUNG READERS • An imprint of Simon & Schuster Children's Publishing Division • 1230 Avenue of the Americas, New York, New York 10020 • Text © 2021 by Alice B. McGinty • Illustrations © 2021 by Diane Goode • Book design by Chloë Foglia © 2021 by Simon & Schuster, Inc. • All rights reserved, including the right of reproduction in whole or in part in any form. • SIMON & SCHUSTER BOOKS FOR YOUNG READERS and related marks are trademarks of Simon & Schuster, Inc. • For information about special discounts for bulk purchases, please contact Simon & Schuster Special Sales at 1-866-506-1949 or business@simonandschuster.com. • The Simon & Schuster Speakers Bureau can bring authors to your live event. For more information or to book an event, contact the Simon & Schuster Speakers Bureau at 1-866-248-3049 or visit our website at www.simonspeakers.com. The text for this book was set in Century Schoolbook. • The illustrations for this book were rendered in pen and ink and watercolors. • Manufactured in China • 0521 SCP • First Edition • 2 4 6 8 10 9 7 5 3 1 • Library of Congress Cataloging-in-Publication Data • Names: McGinty, Alice B., 1963- author. | Goode, Diane, illustrator. • Title: Step by step / Alice B. McGinty ; illustrated by Diane Goode. • Description: First edition. | New York : Simon & Schuster Books for Young Readers, [2021] | "A Paula Wiseman book." | Audience: Ages 4-8. | Audience: Grades K-1. | Summary: On the morning he is to start school, a nervous little boy is reassured by his father's advice to handle problems step by step. • Identifiers: LCCN 2021000029 (print) | LCCN 2021000030 (ebook) | ISBN 9781534479944 (hardcover) | ISBN 9781534479951 (ebook) • Subjects: CYAC: Stories in rhyme. | First day of school—Fiction. | Problem solving—Fiction. • Classification: LCC PZ8.3.M459574 St 2021 (print) | LCC PZ8.3.M459574 (ebook) | DDC [E]—dc23 • LC record available at https://lccn.loc.gov/2021000029LC ebook record available at https://lccn.loc.gov/2021000030

STEP BY STEP

Alice B. McGinty *Diane Goode*

A PAULA WISEMAN BOOK

Simon & Schuster Books for Young Readers

NEW YORK LONDON TORONTO SYDNEY NEW DELHI

Step by step, you learned to walk.
Word by word, you grew to talk.
You're bigger now, and wiser too,
but there's much more in front of you.

What's the way to get it done?
Step by step, one by one.

Piece by piece, you put on clothes.
Insert your legs, your arms . . . your nose.
Pants to shirt, then socks to shoes.
Zip that jacket. Time to cruise.

That's the way to get it done—
pants to jacket, one by one.

Stride by stride, you'll cross the street.
It's loud and wide! It stops your feet!
But move with purpose. One more stride . . .
You made it to the other side!

That's the way to get it done.
Stride by stride, one by one.

Smile by smile, you make new friends.
Maddy, Mia, Luke, Lorenze.

You laugh, you play, you share a toy.
Every smile brings more joy.

That's the way you get it done—
smile by smile, one by one.

Block by block, you build a fort.
It may be strong, but kind of short.

Add a tower. Now it's crowned.
It's MILES high above the ground!

Block by block, one by one,
look at that, you got it done.

Mark by mark, you write your name.
Your letters, though, don't look the same.

Don't give up now. Fill the sheet—
until your writing's clear and neat.

That's the way to get it done—
A to Z, one by one.

One by one, you count to ten.
If you stumble, try again.

Keep on counting. What comes now?
Eleven? Twelve? You did it. Wow!

That's the way to get it done—
counting numbers, one by one.

Word by word, you learn to read.
You start off slowly, then gain speed.
Just sound it out—a word, a phrase.
Soon enough, you've read a page!

Word by word, one by one—
that's the way to get it done.

Kick by kick, you pump the swing.
Lean it. Rock it. Sway. Take wing!
Bend your legs, then whoosh up high.
You'll soon be soaring to the sky.

Kick by kick, one by one,
that's the way to get it done.

Teacher says it's time to clean—
the biggest mess you've ever seen.

But friends together pick things up,
toy by toy, and cup by cup.

That's the way to get it done—
work together. Everyone!

There are even bigger things in store.

More adventures at your door.

Are you ready? Are you prepped?
You can take them step by step!

You KNOW the way to get it done.
Step by step, one by one!